W9-BTR-359

No Sleep for the Sheep!

WRITTEN BY Karen Beaumont
ILLUSTRATED BY Jackie Urbanovic

HARCOURT CHILDREN'S BOOKS
Houghton Mifflin Harcourt | Boston New York | 2011

Harcourt Children's Books is an imprint of Houghton Mifflin Harcourt Publishing Company.
www.hmhbooks.com

The illustrations in this book were done in watercolors
with a brown pencil outline on Arches cold press watercolor paper.
The text type was set in Oneleigh.
The hand-lettering was created by Leah Palmer Preiss.

LIBRARY OF CONGRESS CATALOGING-IN-PUBLICATION DATA
Beaumont, Karen.
No sleep for the sheep! / by Karen Beaumont ; illustrated by Jackie Urbanovic.
p. cm.
Summary: A sheep wants nothing but to go to sleep in the big red barn on the farm,
but each time he closes his eyes, another animal moos or neighs to come in.
ISBN 978-0-15-204969-0
[1. Stories in rhyme. 2. Sleep—Fiction. 3. Domestic animals—Fiction. 4. Animal sounds—Fiction.]
I. Urbanovic, Jackie, ill. II. Title.
PZ8.3.B3845No 2010 [E]—dc22 2009007978

Manufactured in China
LEO 10 9 8 7 6 5 4 3 2 1
4500260783

Sweet dreams and lots of love to my dear friends
Cyndi and Patrick
– K.B.

For my brother Tony and my sister-in-law Barb,
with love
– J.U.

In the big red barn on the farm, on the farm,
in the big red barn on the farm . . .

A sheep fell asleep in the big red barn,
in the big red barn on the farm.

Then there came a loud **QUACK**
at the door, at the door,
and the sheep couldn't sleep any more.

"Go to sleep!" said the sheep
to the duck at the door.
"And please don't QUACK any more!"

"QUACK!" said the duck in the barn.
"Shhh! Not a peep! Go to sleep!" said the sheep
in the big red barn on the farm.

Soon the duck and the sheep fell fast asleep
in the big red barn on the farm.

Then there came a loud **BAAA**
at the door, at the door,
and the sheep couldn't sleep any more.

"Go to sleep!" said the sheep
to the goat at the door.
"And please don't BAAA any more!"

"**BAAA!**" said the goat in the barn.
"Shhh! Not a peep! Go to sleep!" said the sheep
in the big red barn on the farm.

Soon the goat and the sheep fell fast asleep
in the big red barn on the farm.

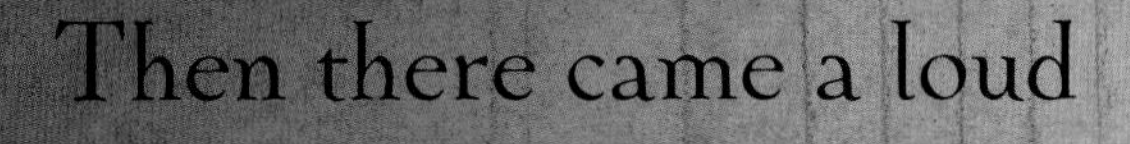
Then there came a loud

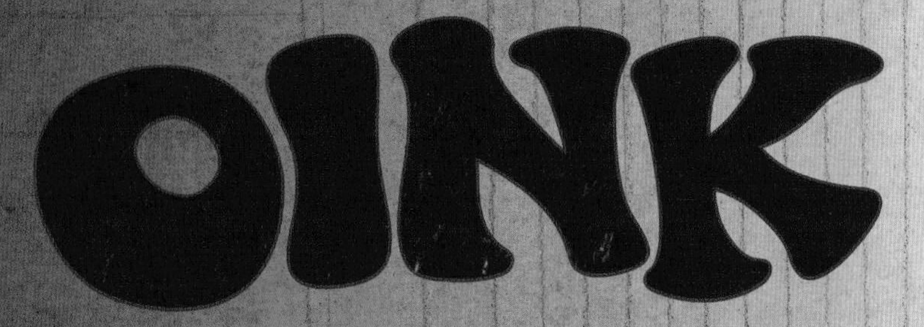

at the door, at the door,
and the sheep couldn't sleep any more.

"Go to sleep!" said the sheep
to the pig at the door.
"And please don't **OINK** any more!"

"**OINK!**" said the pig in the barn.
"Shhh! Not a peep! Go to sleep!" said the sheep
in the big red barn on the farm.

Soon the pig and the sheep fell fast asleep
in the big red barn on the farm.

Then there came a loud

MOO

at the door, at the door,
and the sheep couldn't sleep any more.

“Go to sleep!” said the sheep
to the cow at the door.
“And please don't MOO any more!”

"MOO!" said the cow in the barn.
"Shhh! Not a peep! Go to sleep!" said the sheep
in the big red barn on the farm.

Soon the cow and the sheep fell fast asleep
in the big red barn on the farm.

Then there came a loud

NEIGHHH

at the door, at the door,

and the sheep couldn't sleep any more.

"Go to sleep!" said the sheep

to the horse at the door.

"And please don't NEIGH any more!"

HH

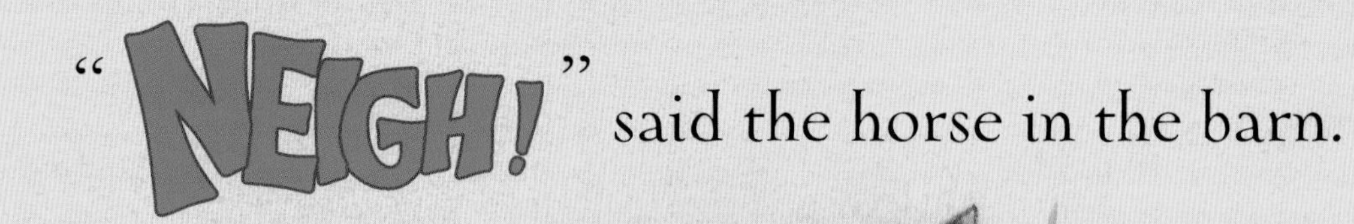

"NEIGH!" said the horse in the barn.

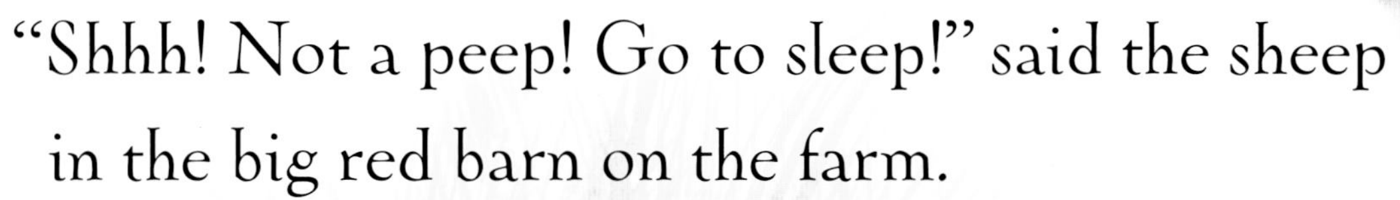

"Shhh! Not a peep! Go to sleep!" said the sheep
in the big red barn on the farm.

Soon the horse and the sheep fell fast asleep
in the big red barn on the farm.

In a deep, deep sleep in the big red barn,
in the big red barn on the farm . . .

Then . . .

COCK-A-

DOODLE-DOO

“Wake up, all of you!
Hey, Sheep! That means you, too!”

Z-Z-Z-Z-Z-Z-Z-Z-Z-Z-Z-Z-Z-Z-Z-Z-Z

But the sheep slept right on through . . .
through the neighs and the moos
and the cock-a-doodle-doos
in the big red barn on the farm.

PEEP!